P9-BYL-766

E   Sharmat, Marjorie
Sha   Weinman

         Hooray for Mother's
         Day!

DATE DUE

HOORAY
for
Mother's Day!

by Marjorie Weinman Sharmat

illustrated by John Wallner

Holiday House / New York

Text copyright © 1986 by Marjorie Weinman Sharmat
Illustrations copyright © 1986 by John C. Wallner
All rights reserved
Printed in the United States of America

Library of Congress Cataloging-in-Publication Data

Sharmat, Marjorie Weinman.
Hooray for Mother's Day!

SUMMARY: In searching for a Mother's Day present
that will be just right for his mother, Alaric Chicken
demonstrates that he is just as cautious and particular
as she is.
[1. Chickens—Fiction. 2. Mother's Day—Fiction.
3. Gifts—Fiction. 4. Mothers and sons—Fiction]
I. Wallner, John C., ill. II. Title.
PZ7.S5299Hn 1986   [E]   85-14146
ISBN 0-8234-0588-5

For my wonderful mom,
ANNA RICHARDSON WEINMAN,
and the annual search
for her perfect present

M.W.S.

For my mom
J.C.W.

Alaric Chicken was very very cautious.

"A chicken can't be too careful," he thought as he got out of bed and looked down to make sure his floor was still there. "What if my floor collapsed in the middle of the night and I stepped down into empty space?"

After breakfast Alaric checked the weather. "Before I go out into the world I have to be prepared," he said. "If it rains I'll need my umbrella and rubber boots. If it's sunny, I can wear my shorts and T-shirt. Unless it's cold and sunny. Cold and sunny is a real problem."

Alaric decided to wear a pair of rubber boots, a pair of shorts and a fur jacket. "Now I am prepared for absolutely anything and everything!" he said.

Alaric went to the telephone and called his friend Lana Pig. "I called to find out what you are doing today."

"Today is Mother's Day," said Lana. "I'm going to visit my mother and give her a present."

"Mother's Day?" asked Alaric. "I have a mother. And I am always prepared for Mother's Day. Today can't be Mother's Day because I am not prepared."

"Well it is," said Lana. "Check your calendar."

Alaric hung up and rushed to his calendar. "What a stupid calendar this is," he said. "It doesn't say Mother's Day on it. But this *is* the second Sunday in May, so it must be Mother's Day. I have to buy a present for my mother."

Alaric went out and locked his door carefully. Then he put up his BEWARE OF VICIOUS DOG and BEWARE OF HUNGRY ALLIGATOR signs. "That should keep away the robbers," he said.

Alaric walked to town. "I must buy a present that's exactly right for my mother," he thought. Alaric went into a department store.

"May I help you?" asked a clerk. "I'm Mrs. Horse."
"I am looking for a Mother's Day present that's exactly
right for my mother," said Alaric.

"How about these lovely bed slippers?" asked Mrs. Horse.

She handed a pair of bed slippers to Alaric.

"Bed slippers?" said Alaric. He looked at them. He sniffed them. He felt them. He blew on them. He gave them back to Mrs. Horse.

"Whoever made these slippers did not think ahead," said Alaric. "They did not think about all the things that can happen to someone wearing bed slippers. These slippers are slippery. My mother could fall and break her bones. These slippers have fuzzy fur. Bits and pieces of it could get between my mother's toes and make her scratch and scratch. She could bleed from all the scratching.

"My mother could end up in the hospital all broken and bloody because of these slippery, fuzzy slippers. This gift will never do."

Alaric walked to the candy department. Mr. Ostrich was in charge. "I see you're looking at our delicious candy," he said. "Would you like to sample a piece?"

Mr. Ostrich handed a chocolate to Alaric. Alaric looked at it, sniffed it, felt it, blew on it and took a tiny bite out of it. He made a face.

"Some of the chocolate is sticking to the roof of my mouth. That can cause cavities. Some of the chocolate is sticking to my wings. This will attract all kinds of loathsome bugs. If I gave this candy to my mother, she would spend half her time at the dentist and the rest of her time slapping bugs. Whoever made this candy was not prepared for the future."

Alaric walked on. He came to the perfume department. "I am looking for a Mother's Day present that's exactly right for my mother," he said to the clerk, Mr. Peacock.

"Oh yes," said Mr. Peacock. "You're the chicken who's making all the trouble. I heard about you from the slippers and candy departments. Well, you can't go wrong with perfume." Mr. Peacock held up a small bottle. "This is very popular with mothers," he said. He handed the bottle to Alaric.

Alaric looked at the bottle. He felt it. He blew on it. "So far, so good," he said. "May I open it?"

"Of course," said Mr. Peacock.

Alaric opened the bottle carefully. He sniffed carefully. "Fumes! They are going up my beak. This perfume could knock me out. It could knock my mother out. It could knock out an entire neighborhood."

Alaric ran out of the store. "This store has terrible presents. Slippers, candy, perfume. Nothing for the kind of mother who likes to be prepared."

Up ahead Alaric saw an artist selling some paintings.

"A painting!" said Alaric. "Something beautiful that will not cause my mother to break bones, bleed, get cavities and sticky wings or keel over from fumes."

Alaric walked up to Ms. Goat, the artist. "Hello. I am looking for a present that will be just right for my mother."

"I have some colorful paintings," said Ms. Goat.

Alaric looked at the paintings. "The colors are too bright," he said. "My mother will need sunglasses to look at these paintings. All of her friends will need sunglasses, too. I will have to buy sunglasses for my mother and all of her friends. I will become poor. I won't have a roof over my head or food to eat or a bed to sleep in. How can you paint pictures that cause so much trouble?"

Ms. Goat shrugged her shoulders. Alaric walked away. He walked up and down the street and in and out of stores. But he couldn't find the right present for his mother. He looked at his watch. "Mother's Day will be over," he thought, "and my mother won't have a present."

At last Alaric came to a pet store. He stopped. He
thought. "That's it! I know the perfect present for my
mother." Alaric went into the pet store. He came out soon
with a huge present wrapped in pretty paper.

Alaric hurried to his mother's house. He walked up the front path. He looked at the signs that said BEWARE OF VICIOUS DOG and BEWARE OF HUNGRY ALLIGATOR. He knocked on his mother's gigantic padlock.

"Who is there?" called his mother. "I don't open doors for strangers. A chicken can't be too careful."

"It's your son Alaric," said Alaric.

"Give me the secret code," said his mother. "If you're my son, you also know that a chicken can't be too careful."

"XCyyy72OOOKNLS," said Alaric. "PXTu3817W."

"That's it," said his mother, and she opened the door.
"Alaric dear, I was just about to go out and visit you," she
said, and she hugged Alaric. Mrs. Chicken was wearing a
pair of rubber boots, a pair of shorts and a fur jacket.

"I brought you a Mother's Day present," said Alaric.
"Here. Happy Mother's Day."

Alaric handed the huge present to his mother.

"Thank you, son," said Mrs. Chicken. "I know you know my taste."

Mrs. Chicken unwrapped her gift. Under the gift wrapping was an . . .

"Another alligator!" said Mrs. Chicken. "Just what I always wanted. Now I can change my sign to read: BEWARE OF TWO HUNGRY ALLIGATORS."

Mrs. Chicken tossed the alligator into the moat that guarded the back of her house.

"Hooray for Mother's Day!" she said. "How do you always manage to pick the perfect present for me, Alaric?"
"Just lucky I guess," said Alaric.